BUNNIES AND THEIR GRANDMA

Pictures by Marie H. Henry
Story by Amy Ehrlich

Dial Books for Young Readers
E. P. Dutton, Inc. / NEW YORK

For my daughter Benedicte
M. H. H.

*For my wonderful
friends at Dial*
A. E.

First published in the United States 1985 by
Dial Books for Young Readers
A Division of E. P. Dutton, Inc.
2 Park Avenue
New York, New York 10016
Originally published by Duculot, Paris-Gembloux 1985
Published simultaneously in Canada by
Fitzhenry & Whiteside Limited, Toronto
©1985 by Duculot Paris-Gembloux
©1985 by Amy Ehrlich for the American text

Printed in Belgium by Offset Printing Van den Bossche
Typography by Atha Tehon
First Edition
COBE
10 9 8 7 6 5 4 3 2 1

Library of Congress Cataloging in Publication Data
Henry, Marie.
Bunnies and their grandma.
Summary: Mother Bunny takes her three children for a day
of fun and games with their cousins at Grandma's house.
1. Children's stories, French. [1. Rabbits—Fiction.
2. Grandmothers—Fiction. 3. Cousins—Fiction.]
I. Ehrlich, Amy, 1942– . II. Title.
PZ7.H3932Bv 1985 [E] 84-20030
ISBN 0-8037-0186-1

The art for each picture consists of a watercolor painting,
which is camera-separated and reproduced in full color.

One morning, bright and early, the mailman brought Mother Bunny a letter.

"For me?" said Mother Bunny. "Why, this looks like Grandma Bunny's handwriting."

"She's invited us to her party. Oh, no, it's today! I must go and tell the children."

"Paulette, Larry, Harry! What's going on in there?"
"Oh, nothing, Mama. Nothing at all."

"We were only fooling around. Please don't punish us," the bunny children pleaded.

"Punish you? I just wanted to show you this invitation from Grandma. We must leave right away."

"Right away! She said *right away!*" cried Paulette, the older bunny sister. "This drawer's a mess. How am I supposed to find anything in here? Ah, my blue sailor dress, my favorite."

Larry and Harry were helping Mother Bunny get ready.

"Here's your hat," said Larry.

"My hat!" exclaimed Mother Bunny. "It didn't look like that *last* year. Perhaps a little mouse chewed up the feather."

"Oh, dear," said Mother Bunny. "It's even worse than I thought. How can I show myself at Grandma Bunny's in this hat?"

"See the scissors?" said Paulette to the bunny brothers. "I think I know a way we can help Mama."

"We can't do that," said Harry.

"Yes, we can," said Larry.

"Good. Then we will. It's settled," Paulette said. "But don't ever tell Mama it was my idea."

Before Mother Bunny had time to get angry, Larry whisked out the scissors again.

"Hmmm, a flower instead of a feather. You know, it just might work," said Mother Bunny.

"It was my idea, of course," bragged Paulette.

"Come on! We were supposed to hurry, remember?" yelled Harry.

The two bunny brothers put on their sailor suits but they weren't very happy about it.

"The ties never stay tied," grumbled Larry.

"Neither do my shoelaces," said Harry.

"Well, if you must know, you both look pretty silly," Paulette said, giggling.

At last, the bunny children and their mother set
out for the party. The morning mist was rising and the
woods smelled fresh and sweet.

Mother Bunny was especially pleased with her new hat. It seemed the perfect thing for a summer day.

"Ah, there you are, my bunnykins!" cried Grandma
Bunny. "How big you've grown! Come and see your
cousins. They've been waiting for you all morning."

"Hey, Harry and Larry!" called the cousins. "Forget that kissing and come play with us!"

Volleyball, jump rope, cowboys and Indians— the possibilities were endless.

As the summer day heated up, so did the little band of bunny cousins. By noon they were ready for something quieter.

"How about croquet?" suggested Paulette. (She was, after all, the oldest.)

The others thought croquet sounded just right.

But soon the croquet game became a fight to the finish between Paulette and Cousin Gregory. (He was, after all, the next to the oldest.) First Gregory accused Paulette of cheating....

Then he slammed her ball into the woods.
The two cousins took aim and came at each other.
Watch out, bunnies!

It was nearly an hour before Gregory emerged from Grandma Bunny's infirmary. His toes throbbed and his head ached, but his pride hurt even more.

"What can I ever do to make it up to you?" asked poor guilty Paulette.

"I'll take your carrot cake for dessert," replied Gregory promptly.

"It's a deal," said Paulette. The two bunny cousins had a good cry and a good hug and vowed to remain friends forever.

At dinner they sat side by side and chanted with the others, "We want cake! We want cake! We want cake!"

"Me first!" cried Sam, the littlest, crawling out from under the table.

But there was plenty of cake to go around. All the bunny cousins had seconds and thirds, and Sam even had fourths.

"Grandma Bunny promised to read us a story after dinner. I'll pick out the book and you can carry it," said Paulette.

"She *would* have to choose the heaviest," grumbled Harry as he staggered into the living room.

Grandma Bunny settled herself in the rocker and called the bunny cousins. "Now, my bunnykins, if you sit still and listen closely, I will tell you the story of a bunny who was nearly as mischievous as you are. His name was Peter Rabbit...."

The sun was setting and it was time for Mother
Bunny and the three bunny children to start for home.
The others looked after them sadly. "Come back
soon, Paulette, and we'll play some more croquet.
I'll miss you," called Cousin Gregory, waving his
white handkerchief.

Mother Bunny had borrowed a wheelbarrow and as the bunny children grew tired, she tucked them in one by one. The evening mist was falling in the woods and she was glad to be wearing her warm shawl and her fine, new hat. "Good night, my little bunnies," she sang softly. "Good night, good night, good night."